Always and Forever

For Ella and Phoebe, Jan and David
A.D.

For George and Beryl,
with love always and forever.
D.G.

ALWAYS AND FOREVER
A PICTURE CORGI BOOK 978 0 552 56765 7

First published in Great Britain by Doubleday,
an imprint of Random House Children's Publishers UK

Doubleday edition published 2003
Picture Corgi edition published 2004
This Picture Corgi edition published 2013
5 7 9 10 8 6 4

Text copyright © Alan Durant, 2003
Illustrations copyright © Debi Gliori , 2003

Picture Corgi Books are published by Random House Children's Publishers UK,
61-63 Uxbridge Road, London W5 5SA

www.randomhousechildrens.co.uk
www.randomhouse.co.uk

Addresses for companies within The Random House Group Limited can be found at:
www.randomhouse.co.uk/offices.htm

THE RANDOM HOUSE GROUP Limited Reg. No. 954009

A CIP catalogue record for this book is available from the British Library.

Printed in China

MIX
Paper from
responsible sources
FSC® C018179
www.fsc.org

Penguin Random House is committed to a sustainable future for our business, our
readers and our planet. This book is made from Forest Stewardship Council® certified paper.

Always and Forever

Debi Gliori
Alan Durant

PICTURE CORGI

Otter, Mole, Fox and Hare
lived together in a house in the woods.
Otter cooked delicious meals.
Mole made and mended.
Hare kept a beautiful garden
of flowers and vegetables.

And Fox?
He worked harder than
anyone. He was always on
hand with a helpful suggestion
and an encouraging word.
To the others he was
the father of the house.
They were a happy family
and loved each other dearly.

But one day, Fox fell ill.
As the leaves started to drop
from the trees, Fox grew thin,
pale and sad.

One morning he went out alone
into the woods and didn't come back.

His family found him,
still and cold,

covered in leaves, beneath an oak tree. With sadness, they carried him home.

They buried Fox by the light of the moon
in his favourite place, under the willow tree.
The tree wept tears over him.
Otter, Mole and Hare cried too,
as they said goodbye.

A wintry sadness settled on the house in the woods.
Fox's family missed him so much.
They felt lost without him.
"He was so wise," said Otter. "Whenever I had
a problem, Fox always gave me good advice."

"He was so clever too," said Mole.
"You could ask Fox anything
and he always knew
the answer."

"He was so kind and loving,"
said Hare. "He was always
there to give you a hug
when you needed one."

Remembering the things
that they loved about Fox
made his family miss him
all the more. Even talking
about him, their hearts ached.
They fell into silence.

And so it continued, sun and moon, moon and sun.
There was only deep sadness in the house in the woods.

Snow came and went.
The trees started to turn green once more.

One afternoon, Squirrel came to visit.

"Where have you been?" she asked. "Your friends have missed you."

"We've been too sad to go out," said Mole.

"We miss Fox too much," said Hare.

"So do we all," said Squirrel. "But life has to go on."

"How can it, without Fox?" said Otter, and he
started to cry. Mole and Hare started crying too.
Squirrel tried to comfort her friends, but they could not
be comforted. They were very pleased to see Squirrel
again, though, and they invited her to stay for dinner.

Otter cooked a proper meal
for the first time in ages.
"This is delicious," said Squirrel.
She sat back in her chair and smiled.
"You know, there's one thing
I don't miss about Fox,
and that's his cooking,"
she said.

"Do you remember that awful
pie he made?"
"Yes," Otter nodded and he smiled
too as he remembered Fox's pie.
The potatoes were barely cooked
and the pastry was burnt to a crisp.
"Fox was a terrible cook,"
Otter said.

"He was a terrible handyman too," said Hare. "Do you remember that time he tried to make a seat, Mole?"

"Yes," said Mole. The seat had fallen apart the first time Fox sat on it. They'd all laughed, especially Fox.

"And what about the time when you were sick, Hare, and Fox did the weeding?" said Mole. "He pulled up all the carrots by mistake!"

They all laughed, remembering these
funny things. It was a long time since
Otter, Mole or Hare had laughed.
Before Fox had fallen ill there had
always been laughter in the house.
Fox had loved to laugh.

"Do you know," Hare said after a while, "I'm going to make a special garden for Fox under the willow tree." She smiled. "I'll plant carrots there."

"And I shall build a garden bench
for us to sit on," said Mole.

"And I shall cook Fox's potato
pie, once a month," said Otter.
"But don't burn it," said Squirrel.
"I won't," said Otter.

Mole, Hare and Otter sat together often on
Mole's bench, in Hare's garden, full of
Otter's pie, recalling happy times.
As they laughed, they felt they could
hear Fox laughing too, as if he was
still there with them.

And in their hearts and their memories
and their laughter, Fox *was* still there,
part of their family, father of the house

. . . always and forever.

If you liked this book, why not try . . .

Also written by Alan Durant:

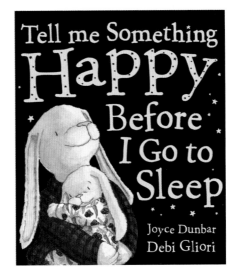

Also illustrated by Debi Gliori: